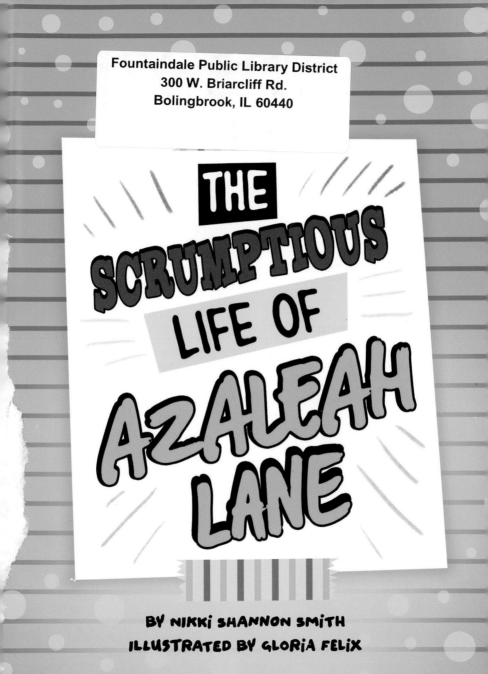

# THE SCRUMPTIOUS LIFE OF AZALEAH LANE

BY NIKKI SHANNON SMITH

ILLUSTRATED BY GLORIA FELIX

PICTURE WINDOW BOOKS
a capstone imprint

Azaleah Lane is published by Picture Window Books,
an imprint of Capstone.
1710 Roe Crest Drive
North Mankato, Minnesota 56003
www.capstonepub.com

Library of Congress Cataloging-in-Publication Data

Names: Smith, Nikki Shannon, 1971- author.
Title: The scrumptious life of Azaleah Lane / by Nikki Shannon Smith.
Description: North Mankato, Minnesota : Picture Window Books, an
imprint of Capstone, [2021] | Series: Azaleah Lane | Audience: Ages
5-7. | Audience: Grades K-1. | Summary: Azaleah and her sisters are
delighted to spend a weekend at Auntie Sam's while their parents
are away, but the cookies Azaleah tries to bake are awful and she is
determined to learn why.
Identifiers: LCCN 2020030332 | ISBN 9781515844662 (hardcover) |
ISBN 9781515844709 (ebook)
Subjects: CYAC: Baking—Fiction. | Aunts—Fiction. | Sisters—Fiction.
| African Americans—Fiction. | Mystery and detective stories.
Classification: LCC PZ7.S6566 Scr 2021 | DDC [Fic]—dc23
LC record available at https://lccn.loc.gov/2020030332

Image Credits: Shutterstock: Beskova Ekaterina, design element
throughout

Designer: Kay Fraser

# TABLE OF CONTENTS

# HEY, THERE! I'M AZALEAH!

I'm eight years old and in the third grade. My life is *amazing*. I live in Washington, D.C., with my family: Mama, Daddy, Nia, and Tiana. Washington, D.C., is our nation's capital and the *coolest* place to grow up.

Mama has her very own restaurant here called Avec Amour. That means "with love" in French. She named it that because she adds love to everything she does.

My daddy is a lawyer. He sues bad guys for a living. The bad guys are big businesses that do things that hurt other people. But my daddy makes them pay. He makes sure they're held responsible.

Tiana is my baby sister. She's four years old and pretty cute—most of the time. I like her a lot, even though she comes in my room too much. I also have an older sister named Nia. She's in middle school and is always in her room. *Always.*

Mama's sister—my Auntie Sam—takes care of us when Mama and Daddy are busy. I love Auntie Sam. She's never too tired to play, and she likes to do art. She also likes adventures—my favorite!

Aside from my family, there are three main things you should know about me.

1. I'm curious . . . *not* nosy. (Despite what Nia says.)

2. I'm good at solving mysteries—very good.

3. I live in the White House!

OK . . . not the *real* White House. (The president of the United States lives there.) But my house is big and white, plus it has a great big living room and a nice backyard. It's just as good as the real White House, if you ask me!

**IT'S HARD TO BELIEVE THIS AMAZING LIFE ALL BELONGS TO ME, AZALEAH LANE!**

# CHAPTER 1

# BON VOYAGE

Usually when I went to Mama's restaurant, Avec Amour, I sat at a table with my sisters and waited for a yummy treat. But today was different. Today we were waiting for Auntie Sam. She was coming to pick us up. We were going to her house for the weekend. I couldn't wait!

I stood at the front window and peeked between the fancy letters painted on the glass. My little sister, Tiana, stood next to me. Her nose was squished against the window. The glass steamed up every time she breathed.

Our big sister, Nia, was at a table studying her lines for her next show. Daddy called Nia a triple threat because she could sing and dance *and* act. Nia was always in a show, and she was always studying her lines.

"There she is!" yelled Tiana. She jumped up and down.

I spotted Auntie Sam walking down the sidewalk and ran to open the door. As soon as she walked in, Tiana wrapped herself around Auntie Sam's leg.

Tiana was holding her leg so tight that Auntie Sam couldn't even walk. She just laughed about it. That's how Auntie Sam was. She almost never got mad.

"Hi, Auntie Sam!" I said.

"Hi, Azaleah," said Auntie Sam. She bent down and kissed my forehead.

Mama hurried out of the kitchen and grabbed the suitcase next to the door. She

set it next to Auntie Sam. Mama was so busy rushing around that she forgot to say hello to her own little sister.

"Tiana, give Auntie Sam her leg back," said Mama. "Azaleah, go get your backpack. Nia, time to go."

Nia looked up from her script. "Auntie Sam! I didn't realize you were here."

Sometimes my big sister didn't pay attention to anything else while she was studying. But I think Nia was just as excited as I was because she smiled and jumped up. She put her script in her backpack and joined us near the door.

Auntie Sam picked up the suitcase and winked at Nia. "I don't think your mama knows I'm here either," she said. "Hello, Tanya."

Mama laughed. "I'm sorry," she said. "Hello, Sammi. I'm just in a hurry to finish here so we can leave."

I knew Mama was excited to get out of town. She and Daddy were going to a food-truck festival for the weekend. Mama was judging the seafood-cooking competition. Daddy was going to spend the whole time eating all kinds of food.

Auntie Sam looked at me. "Well," she said, "are you ready for a weekend in Foggy Bottom?"

Tiana and I giggled. Foggy Bottom—
where Auntie Sam lived—was a silly name
for a neighborhood.

"I can't wait!" I yelled.

We always did all kinds of fun things
when we spent the night with my auntie.
We took walks by the Potomac River and
went out to eat and did arts and crafts. Plus,
Auntie Sam had lots of extra movie channels
on her TV.

"Bon voyage, Mama," I said. That meant
"have a good trip" in French. My teacher
had taught us that.

"Bon voyage, babies," said Mama.
"Be good for Sammi this weekend."

Nia rolled her eyes. She didn't like being
called a baby.

Mama handed us a bag with her special,
homemade cookies inside. They were big, fat
cookies with lots of chocolate chips. She used

her own secret recipe to make them. Then she kissed us each on the cheek.

"Let's go," said Auntie Sam. "This is going to be a great weekend!"

I skipped all the way to Auntie Sam's car. Auntie Sam put our suitcase in the trunk. Then she buckled Tiana into her car seat. I hopped into the back seat too.

On the way to Auntie Sam's house we stopped to get a pizza. At home, we usually had leftovers from Avec Amour for dinner. Auntie Sam didn't cook much, though. She always said Mama was the chef, and she was the artist.

Auntie Sam was an interior decorator. She made people's houses pretty inside. She had even decorated my room for me!

At the pizza place, Auntie Sam let us pick the toppings. My sisters and I agreed on Canadian bacon, sausage, pepperoni, and pineapple. Auntie Sam even got us strawberry soda. Mama and Daddy *never* bought soda. I could already tell this was going to be the best weekend ever.

Auntie Sam got a tiny, flat pizza for herself. I figured she probably wanted her own kind of pizza. She was very picky and didn't like pineapple. She also loved something we didn't: anchovies. *Yuck!*

When the pizza was ready, we drove to Auntie Sam's apartment. She lived in a big, fancy building called Watergate Apartments. The building was shaped like half of a circle and had lots of floors. It also had a shopping center and a nail salon.

The best part was that you could go all the way up to the roof and look down at Washington, D.C. You could even see the river!

As soon as we walked into the apartment, Auntie Sam's dog, Woofer, started jumping all over us. She had to hold the pizza way up high so he wouldn't try to steal it.

"Let's get this party started!" said Auntie Sam. "We can pick a movie and eat in the living room."

Nia ran over to the shelf where Auntie Sam kept her TV remote. She turned on the TV and started checking all the movie channels.

"*Chitty Chitty Bang Bang* is about to start!" yelled Nia. She clapped her hands together and grinned. "That's the next show we're putting on at school! I get to be Truly Scrumptious!"

"Your mama told me," said Auntie Sam. "Congratulations. It's one of my favorite movies."

"Truly Scrumptious isn't the lead," explained Nia. "But it's the part I wanted."

Nia pushed a button on the remote. Auntie Sam handed me a blanket to spread out on the floor. We always had a picnic dinner at her house because her table was only big enough for two people.

Auntie Sam set out plates, napkins, and cups. Then she put Woofer in his crate and put the pizza on the floor.

Tiana plopped down on the blanket. "Showtime!" she yelled.

"Strawberry soda time!" I said.

Nia raised her eyebrows at us. "Truly Scrumptious time," she said in her actor voice.

"What's scrumptious?" asked Tiana.

"It means really delicious," said Nia. "But it's also the lady's name in this show."

"What's the show about?" I asked.

"You're going to like it," said Nia. "It's about a dad and his two kids. They get this old car named Chitty Chitty Bang Bang. Then they meet Truly Scrumptious and go on a magical adventure in the car."

We all loved the movie, and Auntie Sam and Nia sang along to all of the songs.

*This Friday night is just perfect,* I thought. *And I get to eat Mama's scrumptious cookies for dessert!*

That gave me an excellent idea.

"Auntie Sam," I said, "can I please bake some welcome-home cookies to give to Mama and Daddy when they get back?"

Auntie Sam shook her head. "Sorry, Azaleah. I don't keep baking ingredients here. The only thing I have is flour."

I thought for a minute. I really wanted to bake cookies. Mama always said cooking for someone was like giving them a gift. I never got to cook for Mama. She deserved a gift. She always took care of us, and she had to work this whole entire weekend.

"Maybe we could go to the store tomorrow," I suggested.

"Hmm . . . ," said Auntie Sam. "I guess so. That might be a good outing. But right now, it's time for your slumber party!"

"Yay!" yelled Tiana.

My sisters and I changed into pajamas and dragged our sleeping bags into the living room. That's where we always slept when we spent the night. Auntie Sam only had one bedroom.

Mama had offered to let Auntie Sam come to our house instead. That way we could sleep in our own rooms. But we always begged to stay at Auntie Sam's. The slumber party was part of the fun!

Tiana fell asleep right away. Her favorite stuffie, Greenie, was on her face.

Nia turned on her phone's flashlight. We stayed up late and used our hands to make shadow shapes on the wall. But then Nia fell asleep too.

I tried to sleep, but I couldn't. I was too excited about baking cookies. Woofer curled up next to me and fell asleep. I squeezed my eyes shut so tomorrow could come.

# CHAPTER 2

# MORNING STROLL

I was the first person awake on Saturday morning. I tiptoed into Auntie Sam's room. All I could see was her purple bonnet sticking out from under the covers.

I leaned over her head. "Auntie Sam?" I whispered.

She uncovered her face and squinted at me. "What's wrong, Azaleah?"

I thought that was a strange question. "Nothing," I said.

"Why are you up?" she asked.

I giggled. "Because it's morning."

Auntie Sam looked at the clock. Then she looked at me. "It's six-thirty in the morning. You can go back to sleep."

"But we have to go to the store," I said.

Auntie Sam pulled the covers up to her nose. "It's not open yet."

"Oh," I said. "Can I watch cartoons?"

She sighed. "Keep the volume low, okay?"

I nodded and went back to the living room. As soon as the TV turned on, Tiana's eyes popped open. She smiled and slid into my sleeping bag with me. We watched four whole cartoons before Auntie Sam woke up.

Finally, Auntie Sam came out of her room. She peeked at Nia, who was still asleep.

"Ready for breakfast?" Auntie Sam whispered.

"Are we having waffles?" asked Tiana.

"Grits, sausage, and eggs?" I asked.

"Shhh. Oatmeal," said Auntie Sam.

Tiana and I frowned at each other.
We didn't like oatmeal. But we followed
Auntie Sam to the kitchen anyway.

Auntie Sam opened little pouches of
oatmeal and poured them into three bowls.
Then she microwaved a mug of water and
poured it into the bowls. Steam that smelled
like cinnamon drifted to my nose.

"Oh, your oatmeal smells yummy," said
Tiana.

Nia came into the kitchen. Her eyes were still partly closed. I could tell she wasn't very excited about oatmeal either.

Auntie Sam carried the bowls to the living room. She set them on the coffee table and turned off the TV.

I took a bite of oatmeal. "Oh, this is good! It tastes sweet."

Auntie Sam smiled. "It's cinnamon-apple-walnut flavor."

"Are we going to the store after breakfast?" I asked.

Auntie Sam nodded. "Yes, we can go after breakfast."

I was glad oatmeal was fast to make *and* fast to eat. As soon as I finished mine, I ran to get dressed.

From the other room, I heard Auntie Sam talking. "Nia, get dressed so we can walk Woofer and go to the store."

Nia got dressed fast, but Tiana took forever. First, she came out with her pants on backward. She had to go back and turn them around. When she came back to the living room, she had on mismatched shoes.

"Tiana," said Auntie Sam, "your shoes need to match."

"Why?" asked Tiana.

I wanted Auntie Sam to say, "Because I said so." That's what Mama said sometimes if Tiana asked *why* too many times. But Auntie Sam was very patient.

"Shoes are supposed to match," she explained. She pointed at her feet. "My shoes match. See?"

Tiana looked at Auntie's shoes, then mine and Nia's. "Okay," she said. She disappeared back into the bedroom.

I sighed. Even Woofer looked like he was tired of waiting. He flopped down by the door.

When Tiana finally came out again, her shoes matched. But she had put stickers all over her face and arms! We had to peel them off before we could leave.

At first the walk was fun. It was a nice, sunny day. Woofer was wagging his tail. Nia was singing. I was looking in the store

windows. But halfway down the block, Tiana started to whine.

"I'm tired," she said.

"It's okay, we're stopping," said Auntie Sam. She tied Woofer's leash to a pole.

"Why are we stopping?" I asked.

"To get cookie ingredients," said Auntie Sam.

I looked at the building in front of us. There were sunglasses, stuffed animals, and umbrellas in the window.

"But this isn't a grocery store," I said. "This is the kind of store you go to if you need medicine for an ear infection. Or a birthday card for your friend."

Auntie Sam tapped my nose with her finger. "It's a convenience store," she said. "It has some of everything." She opened the door, and we all went in.

"I'm going to go look at the makeup," announced Nia.

"The food is over here," said Auntie Sam. She headed toward an aisle at the side of the store.

"I'm tired," Tiana complained.

"Auntie Sam, this food doesn't look like the kind Mama buys," I said.

Auntie Sam looked at me. "These ingredients will work just fine," she said.

I wasn't sure I believed her. Especially since she didn't cook. Auntie Sam picked up a red-and-white box.

"What's that?" I asked.

"Salt," she said.

"But salt comes in a round container," I explained.

"I'm tired," said Tiana. "Can we go home?"

"Salt is salt," said Auntie Sam, sounding a little bit grumpy. She picked up another red-and-white box.

"What's that?" I asked again.

"Sugar," answered Auntie Sam.

"I don't think that's the right kind," I said, shaking my head. "Our sugar doesn't come in a box. It comes in a bag."

Tiana sat down on the floor and started to cry.

Auntie Sam put the salt and sugar back on the shelf. "We don't have to buy anything," she said. "Let's just go home. We don't have to bake cookies."

"No!" I said quickly. We couldn't go home with *nothing*. Then I wouldn't have a welcome-home gift for Mama and Daddy.

Auntie Sam picked Tiana up off the floor. "Let's go find Nia," she said.

I followed Auntie Sam. I could tell she was irritated. Mama got that way sometimes when we complained a lot. She said it was a certain kind of mad mixed with being

annoyed because something was getting on your nerves.

Auntie Sam never got irritated with us, though.

I already knew Tiana's whining was annoying. And my complaining about the ingredients probably wasn't helping.

Auntie Sam was trying to do something nice, and we were not acting very nice at all. We were ruining our own fun.

"Auntie Sam?" I said quietly. "I'm sorry. Thank you for taking us to the store."

Tiana was still crying. I gave her a serious look. "You need to apologize to Auntie Sam."

"But I'm tired," Tiana whined.

"I know," I said. "But Auntie Sam is doing us a favor. We shouldn't complain."

Tiana looked at Auntie Sam. "I'm sorry," she said.

Auntie Sam smiled at us. "I accept your apology," she said. "Let's get what we need and get out of here."

Auntie Sam got everything we needed for cookies. None of the ingredients looked like Mama's, but I didn't say anything else about it. She also bought Nia some makeup to play around with back at the apartment.

When we got outside, Auntie Sam untied Woofer's leash. "Azaleah, can you hold on to Woofer?"

I took the leash. Auntie Sam gave Tiana a piggyback ride all the way home. Nia and I had to jog a little bit just to keep up. I didn't mind, though. The faster we went, the faster I could start on my cookies.

## CHAPTER 3

# A GOOD SOUS-CHEF

Nia went into the bathroom with her new makeup as soon as we got back to the apartment. I headed straight to the kitchen with the cookie ingredients. Tiana was right behind me.

"Can I help?" she asked.

I really wanted to do it myself, so I said, "You can watch."

Tiana started whining again. "I want to help." She pushed one of the chairs up to the counter. Then she stood on it and started taking the groceries out of the bag.

I didn't want to waste time arguing with Tiana. I let her put everything on the counter. Then I arranged the ingredients on one side of the counter with the front of the boxes showing.

When I was done, I found two big mixing bowls in a cabinet. I put them in the center of the counter. Finally, I found measuring cups and spoons and put them next to the bowls.

"Auntie Sam, where's the flour?" I asked.

Auntie Sam opened a cabinet on the other side of the kitchen. She handed me a full canister labeled *FLOUR*. Then she gave me two empty canisters labeled *SALT* and *SUGAR*.

I put the canisters on the table. When I turned back around, Tiana had rearranged everything on the counter.

"Tiana, stop!" I said.

"I want to help," she said again. She
crossed her arms and poked out her lip.

Auntie Sam stared at us. I remembered
what had happened in the store. If Tiana and
I started arguing, Auntie Sam might give us a
time-out.

Then I got the perfect idea. Sometimes
Mama let me be her sous-chef when she
cooked at home. I was her helper, but she
told me what to do.

"Do you want to be my sous-chef?"
I asked Tiana.

"No," Tiana said right away. Then she
paused. "What's that?"

Auntie Sam chuckled.

"The sous-chef helps with the
ingredients," I explained. "You know
Karen at Avec Amour?"

Tiana nodded. "I like Karen. She's nice.
She lets me taste things sometimes."

"Karen is Mama's sous-chef," I said.

Tiana's eyes got big. "Okay!" she said.
"Can my name be Karen?"

I tried not to laugh. "Okay, Karen.
Are you ready to start?" I asked.

Auntie Sam interrupted us. "Azaleah,
come help me find my apron so you don't
get your clothes dirty."

"I want to wear an apron too!" said
Tiana.

"I only have one," said Auntie Sam. "But we'll get a T-shirt for you to put over your clothes."

"Don't touch anything while I'm gone," I told my sister.

Tiana started to whine, but Auntie Sam stopped her. "Tiana, go sit at the kitchen table until we get back."

Tiana nodded and climbed down from the chair. I followed Auntie Sam to her room.

"Why is your apron in the bedroom?" I asked.

"It was a gift from a client, but I never use it," she said. "It came with those canisters. You check the drawers. It's a yellow apron with chili peppers on it."

I looked through the dresser drawers but didn't find the apron. I closed the last drawer and turned around. Auntie Sam was

standing on her tippy toes in the closet.
She stretched to reach the top shelf.

"Here it is!" she said. "I forgot it came with a chef's hat. Should we let *Karen* wear it?"

We both laughed. Tiana loved to pretend. She was always dressing up at home. Sometimes she was a cowgirl. Sometimes she was a ballerina. Sometimes she put on our old Halloween costumes.

I knew she would really like wearing a chef's hat. Auntie Sam also picked out an old T-shirt for Tiana to wear.

When we went back to the kitchen, I saw that Tiana had been very busy—*not* listening. The canisters were on the counter. Tiana had poured the salt and sugar into them. I could tell because the ingredients were all over the counter.

Auntie Sam looked at the mess. "Oh my goodness." She picked Tiana up and sat her in the chair where she should have been waiting.

"Tiana, what did you do?" I said. "You weren't supposed to touch anything!"

"I'm not Tiana," my sister reminded me. "I'm Karen. And I helped."

Auntie Sam sighed. She cleaned up the mess on the counter so we could start baking. Then she turned the oven on to preheat.

Tiana said, "Are we ready now? Can we put on our chef clothes? Is that a chef hat?"

I nodded and put the hat on her head. It was too big, but Tiana grinned anyway.

"Yes, we're ready now," I said.

I really wished I had Mama's special recipe. Her cookies were the best. Instead, I would have to use the recipe on the back of the chocolate-chip box.

I read the instructions very carefully and followed one step at a time. I measured each

ingredient. Tiana poured it in the bowl.
I even did a good job cracking the eggs
because Mama had taught me how.

The last step was to pour in the chocolate
chips. Tiana and I both ate just one. Even
though they came in a big, weird box, the
chocolate chips tasted good.

When the dough was ready, we scooped
it onto the baking sheet. Auntie Sam came to
look at our work.

"Looks good," she said. "I can't wait to taste them." She put them in the oven for us so we wouldn't burn ourselves.

"Auntie Sam, will you set the microwave timer for ten minutes?" I asked.

"Sure," she said. "Let's color while we wait."

When the timer went off, we jumped up. Auntie Sam took the cookies out for us. She put them on the stove to cool.

I took one look at my cookies and knew something was wrong. They were very, very flat. They had melted and stuck together. They were also way too brown. The edges were almost black. They didn't smell very good either.

"Did we burn them?" I asked.

Auntie Sam examined the cookies. "I don't know. Let's let them cool for a minute or two. Then we can taste them. They might be okay."

"They don't look okay," said Tiana.

I frowned. Tiana was right. We had followed every step, but my cookies didn't look like any other cookies I had ever seen. My cookies looked very, very wrong.

*What did we do wrong?* I wondered.

## CHAPTER 4

# NOT SCRUMPTIOUS!

I stared at the cookies and waited for them to cool. Auntie Sam picked Tiana up and stood next to me.

Nia walked into the kitchen. She had on lipstick, eye shadow, and mascara.

"Um, what's the matter with those cookies?" she asked with a giggle. "They look like dog biscuits."

Tiana started crying. Auntie Sam said, "That's enough, Nia."

Nia stopped laughing, but I could still see her smiling.

"It's not funny," I said.

I didn't know what was wrong with the cookies. But I did know one thing: If food looked bad, people wouldn't eat it. Mama said presentation was important. I didn't want to give Mama nasty-looking cookies.

"Do they taste as bad as they look?" asked Nia.

Auntie Sam gave me a concerned smile. "Let's find out," she suggested. "They should be cool enough now."

She cut the corner cookie away from the other two cookies it was stuck to. Then she cut it into four pieces.

I could tell the cookie was hard because Auntie Sam had to press down on the knife with both hands. Cookies weren't supposed to be that hard.

Auntie Sam, Nia, Tiana, and I each took a piece. We all tasted the cookie.

"Yuck!" yelled Tiana. She spit hers into her hand.

Nia spit hers out too. "Yup," she said. "They do taste as bad as they look."

Auntie Sam chewed and swallowed her cookie, but I could tell she was just being nice. She didn't say anything at all.

I held my cookie in my mouth. It was disgusting, but I was trying to taste what was wrong with it. It was hard, and it tasted as salty as the ocean.

These were the worst cookies I'd ever tasted. They were not scrumptious at all. They were the *opposite* of scrumptious. Even though I didn't want to, I spit mine out too.

I looked at the rest of the horrible cookies. Mama always said that food feeds the body and soul. These cookies weren't even good enough to feed Woofer.

"I don't know what happened,"
I mumbled. "I followed the directions."

I kept my tears inside my eyes and picked
up the baking sheet. Then I walked over to
the corner of the kitchen and dumped the
cookies into the garbage can.

"Now we don't have cookies!" Tiana
cried.

She squirmed out of Auntie Sam's arms
and joined me at the garbage can. Then she
crumbled to the floor, where she cried and
cried and cried.

Sometimes, I thought my little sister cried
too much. But right now, I felt like sitting on
the floor and crying too.

Auntie Sam picked Tiana up. "I think
you need a nap," she said.

"No nap!" yelled Tiana.

"You can sleep in my bed," Auntie Sam
offered.

Auntie Sam was smart. Tiana loved to sleep in other people's rooms. It worked—Tiana laid her head on Auntie Sam's shoulder, and they left the kitchen.

Nia gave me a sad look. "Sorry your cookies are bad," she said. Then her phone rang in the living room, so she left too.

I stood in the middle of the room and looked around. Whatever had gone wrong with the cookies had happened in this kitchen. That meant the solution was in the kitchen too.

I had a mystery on my hands. I just had to solve it.

# CHAPTER 5

# COOKIE DETECTIVE

I was a good detective. I solved mysteries all the time. But I didn't have to be a detective to know that these cookies were *bad.*

I had two hypotheses:

1. The recipe on the convenience-store chocolate chips was no good.

2. The ingredients were no good.

Now I had to find out which one it was.

The big box of chocolate chips was still on the counter. I had already tasted one chocolate chip, so I knew they weren't the problem.

I read the recipe again. "Eggs, butter, sugar, brown sugar, vanilla."

I thought about the times I'd helped Mama bake cookies. We'd used those things too.

I kept reading. "Flour, salt, baking soda."

Those were all normal ingredients too. There was nothing wrong with the recipe.

I thought back to mixing the dough. We had put all those ingredients in. And I had measured very carefully. There was nothing wrong with my baking either.

That meant it was the strange ingredients from the convenience store. I was suspicious of those ingredients anyway. None of them looked like Mama's. The strangest one was the salt that came in a box instead of a round container.

*I wonder if extra-powerful salt is a thing,* I thought. There was only one way to find out. I had to taste it.

I opened the salt canister. I put a tiny pinch in my hand and looked at it very closely. It looked like regular salt.

I licked my hand. It did *not* taste like regular salt. It was sweet!

That didn't make sense. Sweet salt wouldn't make the cookies taste extra salty. But sugar wouldn't make the cookies taste salty either. Sugar made things taste *good*.

I was confused, but I couldn't give up.
A good detective had to investigate everything.
I needed to use the process of elimination.

I pulled the sugar canister closer to me.
I noticed a tiny piece of paper stuck to the side.
I pulled it off. It was part of one of Tiana's
stickers from earlier.

*It probably got stuck to the canister when she*
*filled it,* I realized.

I took a pinch of sugar and put it in my
hand. It looked like regular sugar. I licked
my hand again.

"Ugh!" I said. "Salty sugar? Gross."

Just then, Tiana walked into the kitchen.
"Hi, Azaleah," she said.

Tiana was an interrupter. I didn't want
to be interrupted right now. I needed to
concentrate.

"That was the shortest nap ever," I said.
"What are you doing up?"

"Auntie Sam fell asleep," said Tiana.
"I got lonely. I want to make good cookies."

Then it hit me. The problem wasn't the ingredients. The problem was my sous-chef. *She* had filled the canisters.

"Well, you're not helping with the next batch," I said. "You're the one who ruined the first ones."

Tiana opened her mouth and let out a long, angry cry. "No, I didn't!" she screamed.

"Yes, you did. You mixed up the sugar and salt. You put them in the wrong containers," I snapped. "You made me put a whole bunch of salt in the cookies."

Tiana looked down and tears dripped onto the kitchen floor. Her bottom lip started to shake.

"I'm sorry," she said. "I didn't mean to. I tried to sound out the words. It was too tricky. They both started with *S*."

Tiana's answer made me feel bad. She was just learning to read.

I remembered one time when I accidentally knocked over Daddy's coffee. It spilled all over his work papers.

At first, Daddy was mad, and I thought I was in big trouble. But when I told him I was sorry, he forgave me. He knew I didn't mean to do it.

*Tiana didn't mean to mess up the ingredients either,* I reminded myself.

I bent down in front of Tiana and gave her a big hug. Then I dried her tears. "It's okay," I said. "It was an accident."

I got the sugar box and the salt box and showed them to her. "Do you want to learn a trick?" I asked.

Tiana nodded.

"Say *salt,*" I said. "Say it very slowly."

"*Ssssaaaalllllttt,*" said Tiana.

"Now, instead of thinking about the beginning, think about the end," I explained. "What do you hear at the end of the word *salt*?"

Tiana grinned. "A *T*!" She pointed at the salt box. "That one is the salt!" She grabbed the sugar box next. "*Sugarrrrrrr*. I hear an *R*! Look! There's the *R*!"

"That's really good," I said. I was proud of my sister, and I was proud of myself.

Just then Auntie Sam came into the kitchen. "What's going on in here?" she asked. I could tell she wasn't happy that Tiana had gotten out of bed.

"Guess what?" I said. "I solved the mystery! Tiana accidently switched the salt and sugar. She got confused, but now she can read!"

Tiana grabbed the boxes and showed Auntie Sam. "See!" she yelled. "Salt! Sugar!"

"That's really good!" said Auntie Sam. She kissed Tiana on the forehead.

"Can we bake another batch?" I asked.

"Please?" begged Tiana.

Auntie Sam put her hands on her hips and took a deep breath. I waited for her to answer. She *had* to say yes. It was the only way I would have a gift for Mama.

Auntie Sam stared at us for a long time. Finally, she said, "Azaleah, that was really good detective work."

"Now that I solved the mystery, I can bake good cookies," I said.

"Not right now," said Auntie Sam.

*At least she said "not right now" instead of no,* I thought.

I wanted to make cookies now, but Mama and Daddy had taught me that it was rude to keep asking the same thing over and over again.

I waited to see if Auntie Sam would say anything else. Tiana wasn't as patient.

"Why not?" she asked.

Auntie Sam grinned at us. "Because . . . ," she said, "I have a surprise for you."

# CHAPTER 6

# A NIGHT ON THE TOWN

"Oooo!" yelled Tiana. "What is it?"

"We're going out for a night on the town," explained Auntie Sam. "Early dinner and a show."

Nia must have been eavesdropping because she ran into the kitchen. "A show? What show?" She grinned and looked from face to face.

"The show is a secret," said Auntie Sam. "But you all need to get cleaned up and get dressed."

"We don't have any dressy clothes,"
I reminded her.

Auntie Sam looked excited. "Yes, you
do! I had your mama sneak some into the
suitcase."

"Yay!" Tiana yelled. She clapped her
hands. "Is it my twirly dress?"

"Let's go see," said Auntie Sam. She led
Tiana to her bedroom.

Auntie Sam's surprises were the best!
I was so excited I didn't even mind waiting
to bake more cookies. I had already solved
the mystery. Plus, dinner and a show would
be a lot of fun.

Nia whispered, "I wonder where we're
going. I wonder what kind of show it is."
Then she twirled out of the room.

Auntie Sam only had one bathroom, so
it took a long time for everyone to get ready.
Tiana was the first one dressed. She twirled in

her twirly dress while she waited for us.
She kept getting dizzy and laughing.

Nia sat on Auntie Sam's bed and bounced with excitement. "Can you at least give us a hint about the show?" she asked.

"Nope!" Auntie Sam said with a wink.

By the time we were all dressed, I was really hungry. Between the cookie mystery and Auntie Sam's surprise, we'd forgotten to eat lunch.

We walked a few blocks to an Italian restaurant called Gina's. It had red-and-white checkered tablecloths. It also had pretty red flowers on each table.

As soon as we sat down, a waiter came to our table. "Welcome to Gina's," he said. He put a basket of warm bread and a little dish of butter in the middle of the table.

Nia, Tiana, and I all grabbed bread at the same time. The waiter laughed and handed us menus.

Auntie Sam opened her menu. My sisters and I kept eating bread. Before I knew it, the whole basket of bread was gone.

"I'm sorry, Auntie Sam," I said. "We didn't save you any."

"That's okay. I don't eat bread anyway," she said.

The waiter came back to our table. "Do you need more bread?" he asked.

"No, thank you," said Auntie Sam. "We're ready to order."

Auntie Sam ordered a salad. Nia, Tiana, and I all got spaghetti and meatballs. The whole time we ate our pasta, Nia pestered Auntie Sam.

"Can't you just give us a little hint about the show?" she asked.

"Hmmm . . . ," said Auntie Sam. "It's on a stage. And there are people in it."

Nia laughed. "Can you tell me more than that?"

Auntie Sam said, "The nickname for the theater is the JFK Center."

Even I knew what the JFK Center was. Nia talked about it all the time. It was the John F. Kennedy Center for the Performing Arts. It was the most famous theater in Washington, D.C. Nia's dream was to perform on that stage.

"The JFK Center?" Nia used a voice that was way too loud for a restaurant. "Are you serious?"

"What kind of show is it?" I asked.

"We're seeing a ballet," said Auntie Sam.

This time it was Tiana who yelled.

"Ballerinas? Yay!"

The theater was close enough to walk to, so we headed there right after we finished dinner. The whole way, Tiana pretended to be a ballerina. Nia pretended to be Truly Scrumptious from her show.

The JFK Center was right next to the Potomac River. It was huge and had lots of windows. When we got inside, I couldn't believe my eyes.

"Look at the lights!" I said. All kinds of fancy fixtures were hanging from the ceiling.

"Oooo, pretty," said Tiana.

An usher led us to our seats.

"Front-row seats?" said Nia in a very loud whisper. She grinned at Auntie Sam.

We sat down, and I looked at the program. There were pictures of the dancers next to their names. The show was called *The Folly of Dance*.

"What's folly?" I asked Auntie Sam.

"It means foolishness," she replied.

"What's foolishness?" asked Tiana.

"It means this show is going to be a little bit silly," Auntie Sam explained.

The lights dimmed, and the show started. It really was silly. There were dancers who were trying to be serious, but one of the other dancers kept playing tricks on them. He kept doing silly dances in the middle of the serious ones.

At the very end, there was a big box on the stage. I was sure the silly dancer would jump out, but there was a surprise. One of the serious dancers popped out instead! Then the silly dancer came onto the stage, and they did a silly dance together.

Right after that, there was another really big surprise. The dancers came into the audience!

First they did ballet in the aisles. A dancer with a red tutu and matching ballet shoes danced on the floor right in front of us. Then a dancer with a wand tapped people very softly on the cheek and blew them kisses.

But the biggest surprise came next. The silly dancer picked people from the audience to come onstage with the dancers!

First he picked a lady in the middle of the theater. He walked her to the front. Then he picked a man from the end of our row. Then he picked Nia, Tiana, and *me*!

"Can we please go with them?" I asked Auntie Sam.

She nodded and smiled. "Absolutely!"

The dancers taught us a silly dance, and the whole audience clapped. Nia was really good. She was so good that the dancers told the audience to clap for her a second time. My sister was already getting famous!

Before I knew it, it was time to go home.

"That was *soooo* fun," Nia said as we headed back to Auntie Sam's apartment.

Tiana tried to twirl and walk at the same time. "I'm a real ballerina now!" she said.

"Thank you, Auntie Sam," I said. "That was amazing."

"Yes, it was," she agreed. "You're more than welcome."

We all smiled for the rest of the night. I think I even kept smiling while I was falling asleep. Tomorrow Mama and Daddy would be home. And now that I'd solved the mystery, I would have cookies ready for them.

## CHAPTER 7

# WASTE NOT, WANT NOT

The next morning, I woke up to Auntie Sam opening the blinds in the living room. "Time to get up, sleepyheads," she said. She tapped Tiana's shoulder to wake her up. She gently shook Nia.

"Why are you getting us up early?" I asked.

"It's not early," said Auntie Sam. "I think you guys must have been pooped out from last night. You slept in."

I hopped up. "Oh, no! I still have to bake cookies."

"Let's have breakfast first," Auntie Sam said.

I didn't want to have breakfast first. I needed to start on my cookies. If Mama and Daddy got back early, the cookies wouldn't be ready.

"Auntie Sam, can I *please* make the cookies first?" I begged.

She sighed. "Okay."

"I think I'll eat in the living room while you bake," said Nia. "I saw my favorite strawberry-flavored cereal in the cabinet."

"Can I be the sous-chef again?" asked Tiana.

"Sure," I said.

This time I *wanted* help. I wasn't sure if I could finish in time without it.

We went into the kitchen, and I pulled out all the ingredients. Tiana got out the bowls, measuring cups, and spoons.

Auntie Sam turned on the oven and helped us switch the ingredients. She poured the sugar out of the salt canister and into a bowl. She poured the salt into the salt canister. Then she put the sugar in the sugar canister.

I followed all of the same steps I'd followed yesterday. But this time the salt was really salt, and the sugar was really sugar. I even tasted them to make sure.

When the cookies came out of the oven, I couldn't believe my eyes. They were as flat as pancakes! And they still looked too brown. I hadn't solved the mystery after all.

"Why are they so flat?" I asked. I didn't want to, but I started to cry. "I did everything right."

Tiana patted my arm. "Don't cry, Azaleah," she said.

Nia came back into the kitchen and put her arm around me. She frowned at

the cookies. "They look better than yesterday at least," she said.

Auntie Sam picked up a cookie and took a bite. "They taste great! Nothing's wrong with these cookies."

Nia broke off a little piece of a cookie. "They taste okay," she said.

I tried a little piece of cookie. Nia was right. They were just okay. The texture was wrong.

Mama's cookies were always soft and chewy and a little bit puffy. They were almost like brownies in the middle. These cookies were too crunchy and not even a little bit puffy. I felt like I was chewing granola.

I didn't know what had happened. The cookies should have come out fine this time.

"I don't want them to taste *okay*," I said. "I want them to taste delicious. I want them to look delicious too."

"Good luck," Nia said. "I'm going to practice my lines."

I sat at the table and rested my head on my arm. "Can I try again?" I asked.

Auntie Sam shook her head. "These are perfectly good cookies. We aren't wasting them, and we aren't wasting any more ingredients."

I sighed. I couldn't give these cookies to Mama. I had to think of a way to make them look *and* taste better.

Just then, I had an idea. I had seen some frosting when I was looking through Auntie Sam's cabinets yesterday. Maybe I could frost the cookies!

"Can I use your frosting?" I asked my auntie. "Maybe that will fix the cookies."

Auntie Sam looked like she felt sorry for me. She got the frosting out and handed it to me. Then she put the cookies on a plate

and brought them to me. She gave me a little
plastic knife too.

"Thank you," I said.

Tiana leaned over the table next to me.
I spread the pink frosting on a cookie.

"Good job, Azaleah," she said.

"It looks better, doesn't it?" I asked.

Tiana nodded. "It's pretty."

Now that I had fixed the presentation,
it was time for a taste test. Mama said you

should always taste your food before giving it to someone else. That way you could make sure it was good.

I cut the cookie in half and gave Tiana the first bite. "Here," I said. "You try it."

Tiana took a great big bite of the cookie. She tilted her head to one side. She chewed and swallowed, but she didn't say anything.

"Is it good?" I asked.

"I don't know," she said. "You taste it."

I took a bite of my half. "No," I said. "It is *not* good. It's gross. Chocolate-chip cookies and strawberry frosting don't go together at all."

I put the plate of unfrosted cookies on the counter. "Auntie Sam, you can have these," I said. "I know you like them, but I don't think Mama will."

Tiana licked the frosting off her half of the cookie. Then she ate the rest.

"Let's eat breakfast," said Auntie Sam.
"It's getting late. Your mama won't be happy
if I forget *two* meals while you're with me."

Even though I knew it was rude to keep
asking, I decided to try one more time. A
good detective never gave up.

"Can I please try one last time?" I asked
Auntie Sam. "Mama always makes good food
for us. She says it's a gift. That means she
gives us a gift every single day. I just want
to give her a gift this time."

Auntie Sam opened the refrigerator to get
the milk. When her head came back out, her
face looked extra tired.

*Maybe our night on the town pooped her out
too,* I thought.

"You sure do have a one-track mind,"
said Auntie Sam.

Auntie Sam was right. I did have a
one-track mind today. I could not stop

thinking about cookies. Giving up on them meant giving up on the mystery too. And I never gave up on a mystery.

I had to find a solution and change Auntie Sam's mind—*fast*.

# CHAPTER 8
# ONE-TRACK MIND

Auntie Sam put the milk and three boxes of cereal on the table. She had gotten a box of everyone's favorite kind.

Tiana liked chocolate-flake cereal. She picked up her box and read it. "Chocolate Flakes." She put her finger on one of the words and sounded it out. "*Yum . . . my.*"

"Close," I said. "That looks like *my,* but that *Y* says *eeee.*"

Tiana tried again. "*Yum . . . eee.* Yummy!" She laughed. "It really is yummy!"

My favorite cereal was called Fruity Circles.
I filled my bowl all the way to the top.

"Thanks, Auntie Sam," I said. "I love this
kind!"

Auntie Sam opened her cereal. It did not
look very yummy.

Tiana read Auntie Sam's box. "*Rye . . . ceee* dots," she read. "Ricey Dots!" I was impressed she'd figured out that the *Y* said *eeee* all by herself.

Auntie Sam poured her cereal and put the box back on the table. Ricey Dots weren't colorful at all. They were shaped like macaroni. I wondered if they tasted like rice.

Tiana kept reading. "*Gluh . . . tennn . . . freeee,*" she said.

"That's pretty good," said Auntie Sam. "But the *U* says *oooo.*"

Tiana tried again. "*Glooo . . . tennn . . . free,*" she read slowly. "Gluten free?"

"What's gluten free?" I asked.

"Gluten is something found in wheat," said Auntie Sam. "It upsets my stomach, so I don't eat it. Gluten free means it doesn't have any gluten."

"Does my cereal have gluten?" asked Tiana.

"Yes," said Auntie Sam.

"It doesn't hurt *my* tummy," said Tiana. Then she shoved a big spoonful of cereal into her mouth.

"What else has gluten?" I asked.

"Lots of things," Auntie Sam said. "Bread, biscuits, pancakes . . . gluten is everywhere."

"Is that why you never eat Mama's biscuits?" I asked.

Auntie Sam nodded and ate her cereal.

"Or any bread last night?" I asked.

Auntie Sam nodded again. I felt bad for her. She couldn't eat a lot of really good foods. She seemed like she liked her cereal, though.

After breakfast, I put my dishes in the sink. Auntie Sam went into the living room with a big cup of coffee. Tiana went with her, carrying a cereal box to read.

I leaned against the counter and thought about my cookies. Since I had a one-track mind, maybe I could use it to solve this flat, crunchy cookie mystery.

I walked over to the oven. It was still on from earlier.

*Maybe it was too hot*, I thought. *Maybe it melted the cookies.*

I looked at the numbers on the dial. Mama had shown me how to read the temperature.

The cookie directions had said, *Bake at 350 degrees.* The oven was set to that temperature. The oven was not the problem.

I sighed and turned it off like Mama always did when she finished baking.

*If the problem isn't me or the recipe or the oven or the ingredients, then what can it be?* I wondered.

Then I realized something very important. I hadn't investigated *all* the ingredients! I had stopped after I noticed the salt and sugar were switched.

*What if there was something wrong with one of the other ingredients?*

I ran to the garbage can. I wanted to check all of the packages. Maybe we'd accidentally bought the wrong thing.

I pulled everything out of the garbage can, but every package I checked looked right. The salt box said *SALT*. The sugar box said *SUGAR*.

Next, I ran to the refrigerator to check the butter and eggs. The butter said *BUTTER*.

The eggs said *Grade AA EGGS*. I didn't know why eggs got grades, but they were the same kind Mama bought.

I was running out of ideas. I had checked every last ingredient that Auntie Sam bought.

*Wait,* I realized. *I checked the things we* bought. *I didn't check the flour because it was already in the canister!*

I walked into the living room. "Auntie Sam?" I said.

"Hmmm?" she said. She was sipping her coffee. Her mug was so big it covered most of her face.

"Is your flour old?" I asked.

Auntie Sam put down her mug and shook her head. "No. Your mama gave it to me a couple of months ago. But flour takes much longer than that to go bad."

The flour couldn't be the problem then. I was running out of ideas.

"What time are Mama and Daddy coming home?" I asked.

"Three o'clock," said Auntie Sam.

I went back to the kitchen and sat at the table. The clock on the wall said twelve o'clock. That meant I had three hours to do three things:

1. Solve the cookie mystery
2. Convince Auntie Sam to let me try again
3. Bake more cookies

Most of the time, it took me longer than three hours to solve a mystery. I hoped my one-track mind also had a very fast train on its track.

# CHAPTER 9

# HURRY UP!

I watched the second hand on the clock. It went round and round, just like my brain. I kept thinking the same thing—the problem *had* to be the ingredients. But nothing was *wrong* with the ingredients.

I was trying to concentrate, but loud laughing kept interrupting me. It was coming from the living room, so I went to see what was happening in there.

Nia was pretending to be Truly Scrumptious. She had a face full of makeup. She was singing the "Toot Sweets" song from *Chitty Chitty Bang Bang*.

Tiana was dancing around in her twirly dress. "Toot! Toot!" she sang in a very loud voice.

Auntie Sam clapped every time Tiana said *toot*. I sat down. I wanted to talk to them about the mystery, but I didn't want to ruin their fun.

When the song was over, Auntie Sam yelled, "Bravo! Encore!"

*Encore* meant "again." When the audience yelled encore, the performers had to do more performing. This show was *never* going to end.

I looked at the clock on the wall. It was twelve-thirty.

"Excuse me," I said. "Do you think you can help me with the mystery?"

Auntie Sam sighed. "Azaleah, please. Let's just enjoy the time we have before your parents get here."

I curled up on the sofa. Tiana moved a chair to the middle of the living room and started to do a silly dance. I knew she was trying to be like the silly dancer from the show.

Tiana kept hiding behind the chair and popping out. I pretended like I was watching, but I was really thinking.

Auntie Sam, Tiana, and Nia were cracking up. They were being so silly I couldn't think.

"I'll be back," I said. Nobody answered.

I went to the kitchen and stared at the cereal boxes we had left on the table. Auntie Sam's gluten-free cereal looked so plain next to mine.

Poor Auntie Sam couldn't eat biscuits or bread or pancakes or any other yummy stuff. She couldn't eat anything with wheat. Not even cereal.

Inside of my head, my brain yelled *wheat!*

All the things Auntie Sam couldn't eat were made from wheat. I knew that *flour* was made from wheat because Mama had told me.

One time when I helped her cook she'd used flour that looked kind of brown. I'd asked her why. Flour was supposed to be white. Mama had explained it was whole-wheat flour.

*But if Auntie Sam can't eat flour, how come she eats cookies?* I wondered.

My one-track mind was trying to tell me something.

1. Yesterday, the salt and sugar canisters said one thing but actually had something different inside.

2. Auntie Sam's cereal box looked like a regular cereal box, but it had something different inside.

*What if Auntie Sam's flour* looks *like flour, but has something different inside?* asked my one-track mind.

I ran to the living room. "Auntie Sam!" I yelled.

The show stopped, and they all stared at me. "What is it, Azaleah?" Auntie Sam said.

"Is your flour really flour?" I asked.

"Yes, it's really flour," said Auntie Sam.
She had a tiny frown on her face.

"Then why doesn't it upset your stomach?"
I asked. "Flour is made out of wheat."

"Mine isn't. It's gluten-free flour," Auntie
Sam explained. Then she got a very strange
look on her face. Her eyes got very big, and
her mouth was shaped like an O.

"The cookies are flat because of the *flour*!" I yelled.

"Oh my goodness," said Auntie Sam. "I'm so sorry. I didn't even think about that. I'm so used to eating gluten-free cookies . . . those seemed normal to me."

"Does your flour make things flat?" I asked.

"Maybe," said Auntie Sam. "I don't really bake, but gluten-free things are always a little bit different than things made with wheat flour."

"I solved the mystery!" I yelled. "I did it!"

I looked at the clock. It was exactly one o'clock. Step one had been to solve the cookie mystery. Now I had two steps and two hours left.

"Can I please try again?" I asked. "With regular flour?"

"I wish you could," said Auntie Sam. "I don't have any regular flour, though."

"Does the convenience store have it?"
I asked.

This time Auntie Sam looked at the clock. "I don't think we have time. We still need to clean up, get dressed, and pack up your things," she said. "Your parents want you to be ready when they get here. Your mama said Nia has homework, and you need your hair washed."

"We can do it. We just have to go fast," I said.

"I'll help!" said Tiana.

"Me too," said Nia.

Auntie Sam stood up. "Okay," she said. "Let's do it. This will be a fun challenge!" She grabbed Tiana's hand and took her to get dressed.

Nia started putting away our sleeping bags and pillows. I ran into the kitchen and put the breakfast bowls and spoons in the dishwasher.

Then I put the cereal away and washed the cookie dishes so they would be ready.

Finally I set out all the ingredients on the counter. But I did *not* take out Auntie's flour.

We all worked so fast, we were ready to leave at one-thirty. Auntie Sam didn't even make Nia wash off her Truly Scrumptious makeup. Now we just had to get to the store and back by two o'clock for step three.

# CHAPTER 10

# TRULY SCRUMPTIOUS

We all walked down the street as fast as we could. Woofer thought it was funny. He kept running around us, which did *not* help us go faster.

When we got to the convenience store, Auntie Sam handed Nia some money. "Tiana and I will stay here with Woofer," she said. "Nia, help Azaleah get regular flour."

"Okay!" said Nia. She grabbed my hand, and we ran into the store.

I remembered exactly where the food was. I pulled Nia to the right aisle. Nia found the flour. I checked to make sure it didn't say gluten-free. Then we hurried to the front of the store, paid for the flour, and ran back out.

Auntie Sam double-checked that the flour was the right kind. Then we all speed-walked back to her apartment. We got back at exactly two o'clock and were all out of breath.

Nia got the butter and eggs out of the refrigerator. Auntie Sam turned on the oven. I put on my apron, and Tiana, my sous-chef, put on her hat and T-shirt.

"Okay, Karen," I said to Tiana. "Are you ready to make cookies?"

"Yes, ma'am!" yelled Tiana.

By now we all knew exactly what to do. We mixed up the dough and plopped little mounds onto the baking sheet. Then Auntie Sam put the cookies in the oven and set the timer.

I stared through the oven window for ten minutes. When the timer rang, Auntie Sam took out the cookies.

"They look really good!" I said.

This time the cookies hadn't melted together. They'd even puffed up a tiny bit.

"They aren't flat!" said Tiana.

Just then the phone rang. "Hello?" said Auntie Sam. "Yes, send them up. Thank you." Then she hung up.

"Who was that?" I asked.

"That was the front desk. Your parents are here early," said Auntie Sam. "They're on their way up."

I looked at the clock. It was only two forty-five. "We barely made it!" I said.

A minute later, there was a knock at the door. We all ran to let Mama and Daddy in. They hugged and kissed us.

"We missed you!" said Mama.

"How was the food-truck festival?" Auntie Sam asked.

Mama smiled. "It was good."

"*Really* good," said Daddy, patting his stomach. He handed each of us a bag. "We got you some souvenirs."

Mama sniffed the air. "Something smells good. Have you been baking?"

Auntie Sam laughed. "We've been baking and baking and *baking*," she said.

"Well let's see the finished product," said Mama.

I hurried to the kitchen and put my cookies on a plate. Then I brought them to the living room.

"I baked these just for you," I told Mama and Daddy.

They each took a cookie, and I realized I hadn't tasted them yet! I waited to see what they would say.

"Mmmm," said Daddy.

"They're delicious," said Mama. "And still warm."

Auntie Sam disappeared into the kitchen. She came back with napkins, milk, and cups. Then she made another trip and came back with a plate of gluten-free cookies for herself.

"Wow!" said Mama. "You even made some for Auntie Sam?"

"Sort of," I said.

Auntie Sam giggled. I told Mama all about my cookie mystery.

Mama shook her head. "I thought you all knew Auntie Sam didn't eat gluten."

"Detective Azaleah solves another mystery," said Daddy. "It's a good thing too. Flat, salty cookies don't sound very good."

"They weren't good at all," I agreed.

"Open your souvenirs," said Mama.

Auntie Sam opened hers first. She got a
bag full of gluten-free treats from the food-
truck festival. Nia got a T-shirt that said *Clap
for me! I'm food-truck famous.* Tiana got a hat
shaped like a taco. She took off her chef's hat
and put it on.

I opened my present last. It was a book.
*"Ten Recipes for Kids and the Mysteries Behind*

*Them*," I read. "I can't wait to read this.
Thank you!"

Daddy grabbed another cookie. "These are
delicious."

"They're scrumptious!" yelled Tiana.

"They're better than that," I said. "They're
truly scrumptious!"

# About the Author

Nikki Shannon Smith is from Oakland, California, but she now lives in the Central Valley with her husband and two children. She has worked in elementary education for more than twenty-five years and writes everything from picture books to young adult novels. When she's not busy with family, work, or writing, she loves to visit the coast. The first thing she packs in her suitcase is always a book.

# About the Illustrator

Gloria Félix was born and raised in Uruapan, a beautiful, small city in Michoacán, Mexico. Her home is one of her biggest inspirations when it comes to art. Her favorite things to do growing up were drawing, watching cartoons, and eating, which still are some of her favorite things to do. Gloria currently lives and paints in Los Angeles, California.

# Glossary

**audience** (AW-dee-uhns)—people who watch or listen to a play, movie, or show

**client** (KLY-uhnt)—a customer

**convenience** (kuhn-VEEN-yunts)—designed for quick and easy use

**eavesdropping** (EEVS-drop-ing)—secretly listening to something private

**encore** (AHN-kor)—a demand by an audience for a performance to be continued or repeated

**fixture** (FIKS-cher)—something, such as lights or a sink, attached as a permanent part

**folly** (FOL-ee)—foolish or silly

**gluten** (GLOO-ten)—a substance in wheat and flour that holds dough together

**hypotheses** (hye-POTH-uh-seez)—ideas about how or why something happens; you can test your ideas to see if they are right

**ingredients** (in-GREE-dee-uhnts)—the different things that go into a mixture

preheat (pre-HEET)—to turn an oven on before you use it; it usually takes about 15 minutes to preheat an oven

presentation (prez-uhn-TAY-shuhn)—the way something is arranged or designed

process of elimination (PROS-es of i-li-muh-NAY-shuhn)—the act of considering and rejecting each possible choice until only one is left

recipe (RESS-i-pee)—directions for making and cooking food

scrumptious (SKRUHMP-shuhs)—delicious

sous (soo)—being an assistant, like a sous-chef

souvenir (soo-vuh-NIHR)—something that is a reminder of a special event

texture (TEKS-chur)—the way something feels

usher (UHSH-er)—a person who leads people to their seats

# Let's Talk!

1. Some treats are sweet and some are salty. Azaleah's cookies were supposed to be sweet, but they came out salty at first. Is your favorite treat sweet, salty, or a combination of the two? What is it? Why do you like it?

2. Azaleah and her sisters got to see a live show at the theater. Tell someone about a live show you've seen. It can be a show you saw at a theater, at school, at a festival, church, or anywhere else.

3. Mama's chocolate-chip cookies are a secret recipe. Think of a food someone makes for you that you really like. Talk to the person who makes it. Ask them what the ingredients are and how they make it. Do they have any "secrets" that make their recipe special?

4. Mama says cooking for someone is like giving them a gift. She says it feeds their body and soul. What do you think she means by that? Do you agree? Why or why not?

# Let's Write!

1. Imagine that you are Azaleah, Nia, or Tiana and are staying at Auntie Sam's house. Write a letter to Mama or Daddy while they are away. Use details from the book to tell them all about your stay.

2. There are lots of people, like Auntie Sam, who can't eat gluten. Learn more about foods that are gluten-free. (You can ask an adult to help you do research on the internet. You can also check the labels on foods you have at home.) Then make a list of at least five things Auntie Sam could eat if she were hungry.

3. In this book, Tiana was Azaleah's sous-chef. Imagine you get to be someone's sous-chef. Write a paragraph telling who you would help, why you picked them, what you would make, and why.

4. Azaleah struggles with her cookie baking, and it takes her three tries to get it right. Write about a time you struggled to do something. What were you trying to accomplish? What challenges did you face? Did you succeed? Why or why not?

# Make Azaleah's Chocolate-Chip Cookies!

Make scrumptious chocolate-chip cookies, just like Azaleah made for Mama and Daddy. You can even share them with someone as a gift. Be sure you have everything on the list and ask an adult before you start baking. If you don't, go to the grocery store or the convenience store.

## What You'll Need:

- 2 ¼ cups flour (you can use all-purpose or gluten-free)
- 1 tsp. baking soda
- 1 tsp. salt
- 1 cup butter (2 sticks)
- ¾ cup granulated sugar
- ¾ cup brown sugar (Tip: Make sure the brown sugar is packed when you measure it. That means you have to mash it down with the back of a spoon until it's nice and flat.)
- 1 tsp. vanilla extract
- 2 eggs
- 2 cups chocolate chips
- mixing bowls
- measuring cups and spoons
- baking sheet
- milk to drink with your cookies! (optional)

## What To Do:

1. Wash your hands and have a grown-up help you preheat the oven to 350°F. Then take out a medium-sized bowl, a large bowl, measuring cups, measuring spoons, a regular spoon for scooping, and a baking sheet. If you want, put on an apron.

2. Mix flour, baking soda, and salt in a medium-sized bowl. (Tip: Use the edge of a butter knife to swipe the extra flour off the top of the measuring cup. It should be flat. It should not look like a little hill on top.)

3. Set the medium-sized bowl off to the side. In the large bowl, beat the butter until it's nice and creamy. Then add both kinds of sugar and the vanilla extract. Mix everything together until it's blended and smooth. (Tip: The butter will be easier to mix if it's soft. You can do that by leaving it on the counter for a few hours. Or you can slice it up and microwave it for a few seconds.)

4. Crack one egg into the large bowl and blend it in. Then crack the second egg into the large bowl and blend it in.

5. Add the dry ingredients from the medium-sized bowl into the large bowl. You have to add it a little bit at a time, and blend it. Then add more, and blend it. Keep doing that until the medium-sized bowl is empty.
6. Stir in the chocolate chips. If you want nuts in your cookies, stir them in now too.
7. Now you're ready to put the cookie dough on the baking sheet. Use a spoon to pick up a small scoop of dough. Drop it on the baking sheet. Repeat until your baking sheet is full. Make sure to leave room between your scoops so your cookies don't stick together.
8. Ask a grown-up to help you put your cookies in the oven. Set a timer for 8–10 minutes. (All ovens are different, so peek at your cookies after about 8 minutes. Burnt cookies are not scrumptious!)
9. When your cookies are ready, have a grown-up take them out of the oven. Let them cool for a couple of minutes on the sheet. Then use a spatula to place them on a cooling rack or plate.

Cookies are truly scrumptious when they are still warm! Eat a warm cookie and drink a glass of milk.

**TiP:** You can make this recipe gluten-free for people like Auntie Sam who can't eat gluten. All you have to do is use gluten-free flour instead of regular flour. If your tummy is very, very sensitive, you should also buy gluten-free vanilla extract.